Written and illustrated by
Philippa Davies

Smidge
and
the Mountain
M ∴ bles

Grosvenor House
Publishing Limited

The Mountain MoOobles lived beyond the very highest ridge

Of a multi-coloured hillside you could only reach by bridge.

The bridge was made from twigs and twine and sunshine-dappled leaves

That flapped and swayed and bounced about in the gusty mountain breeze.

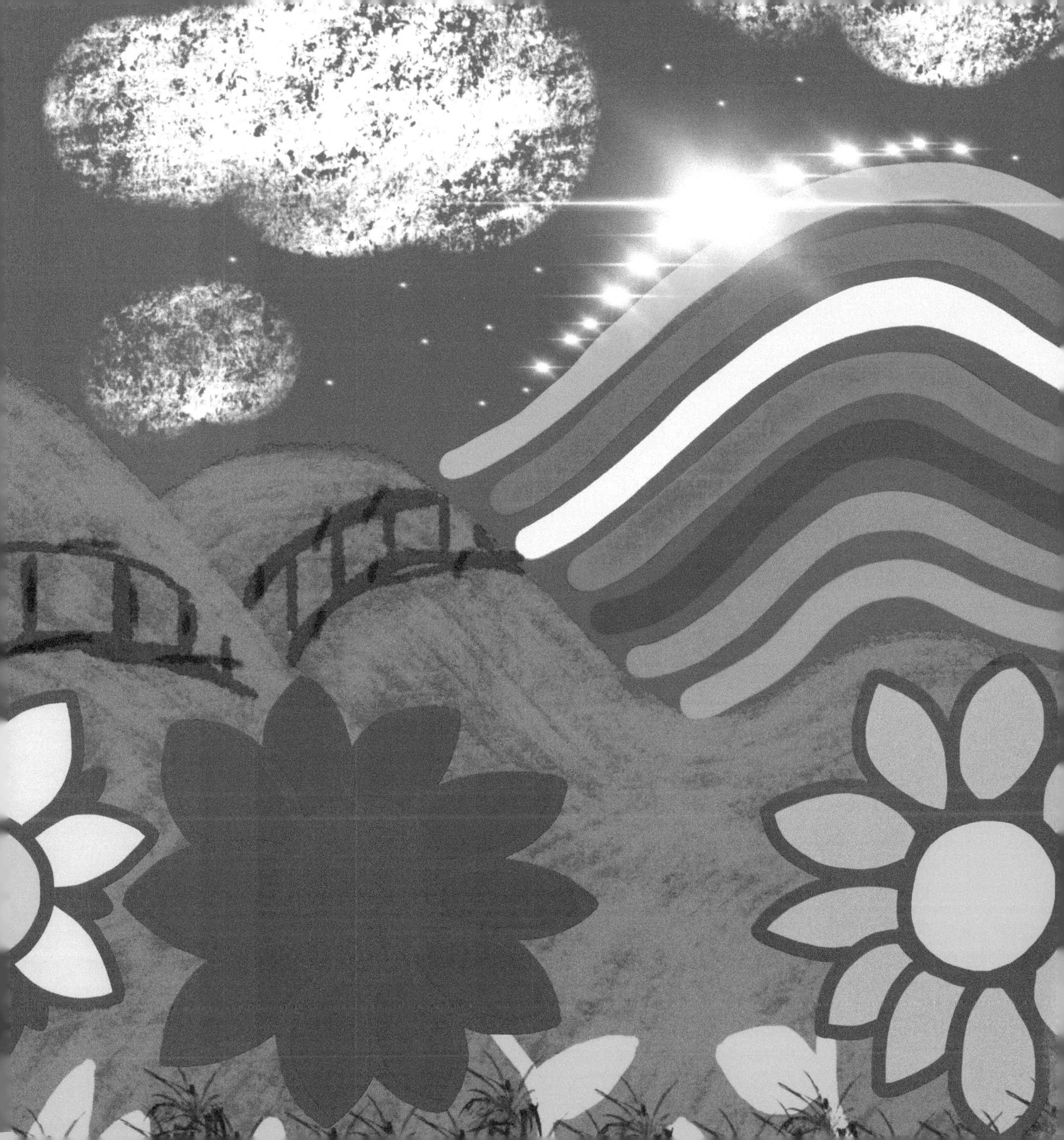

Every day the sun popped up and made the flowers smile

While dew drops sparkled in the light and all in single file

The Mountain MoOobles made their way across the bouncy bridge

In search of rocks to climb and scale – and a giant known as Smidge.

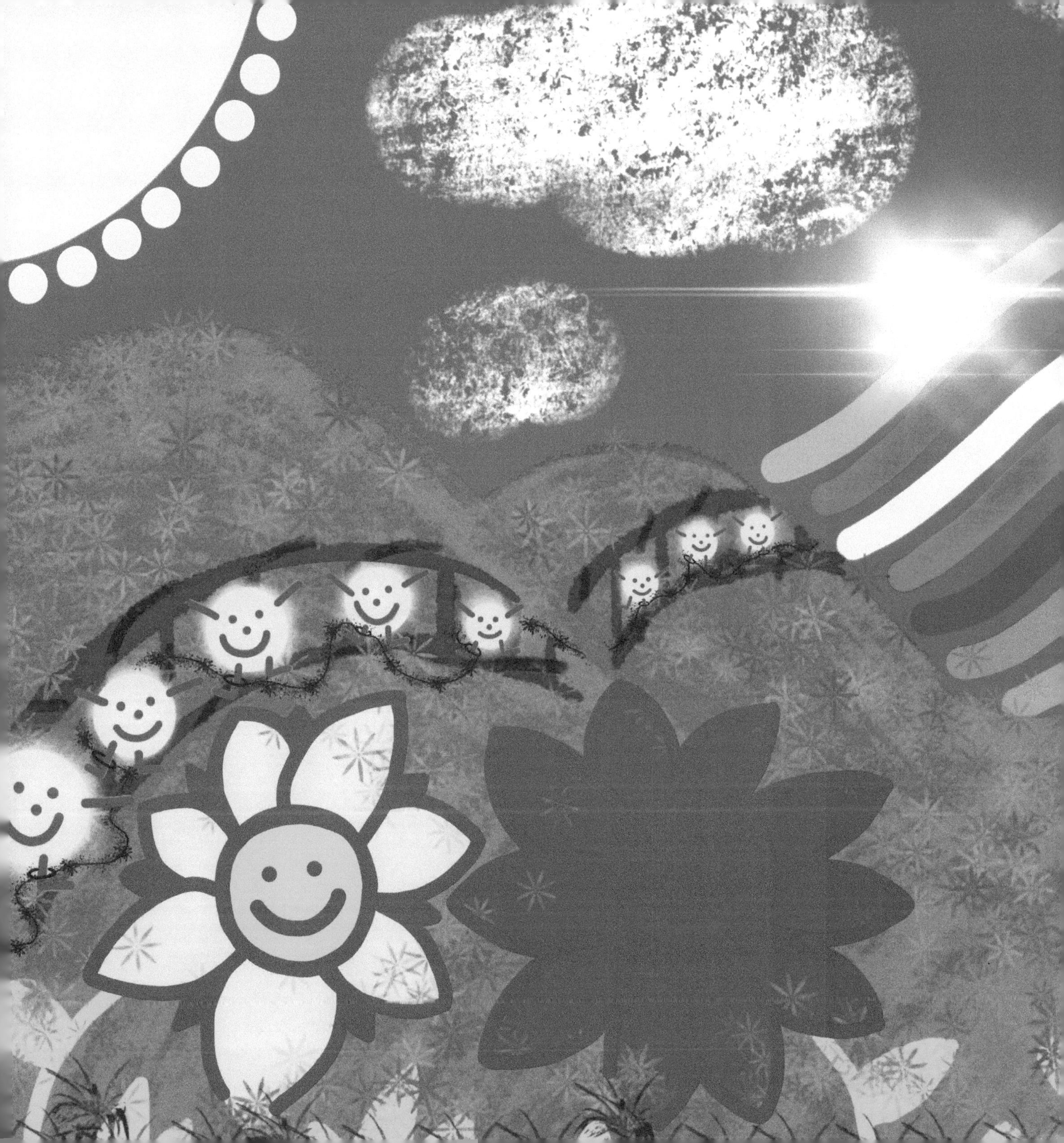

Smidge was a hilltop nomad, who roamed from place to place.

He'd not been seen for some time now, but they all knew his face.

For Smidge was Lord Protector of a very special key

That the Mountain MoOobles needed to set their people free.

They were tied together with the very strongest twine

Made from the roots of mighty oak trees growing tall and fine.

It was Smidge who bound the MoOobles to stop them straying far from home

Because he knew the dangers of going it alone…

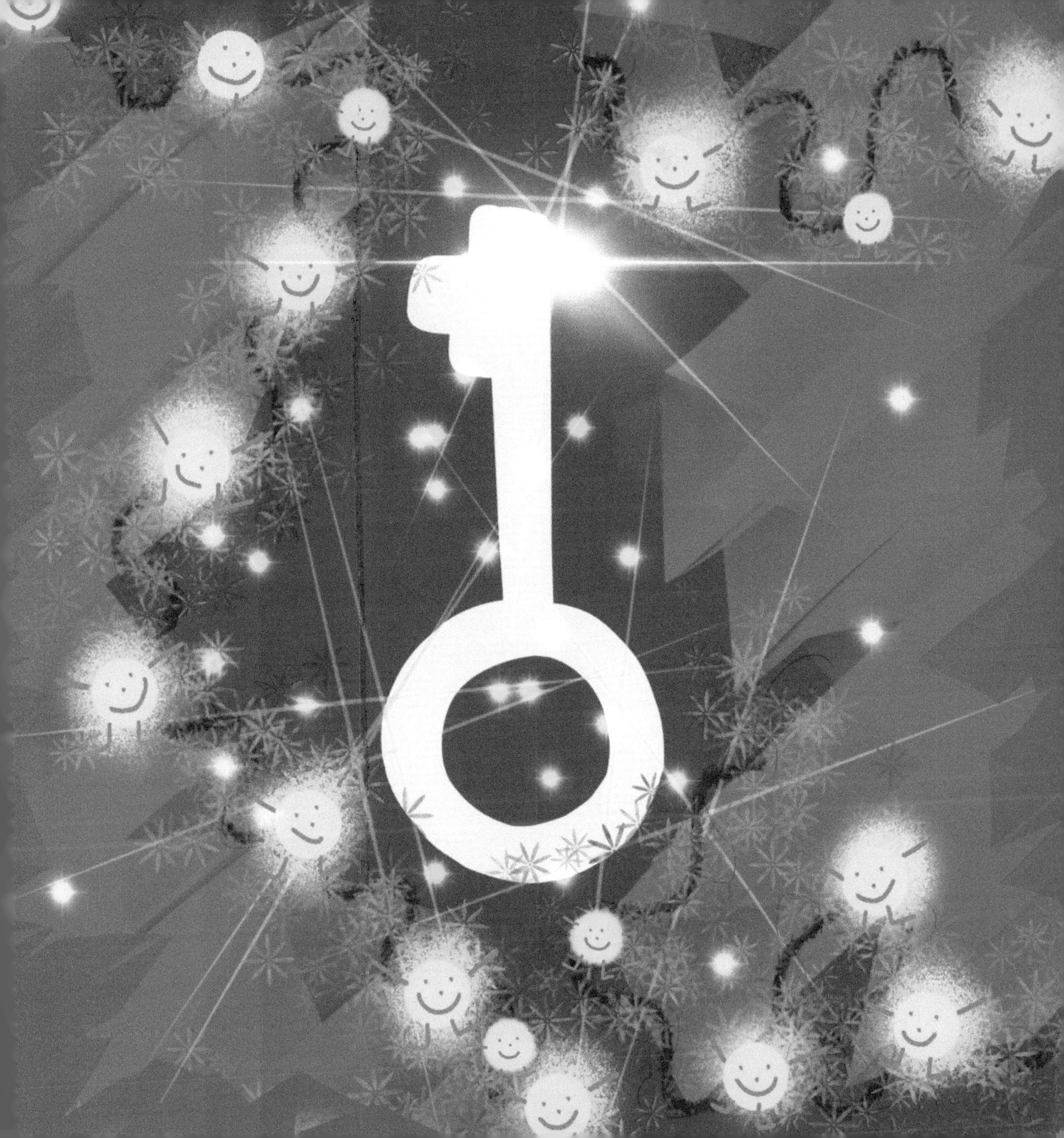

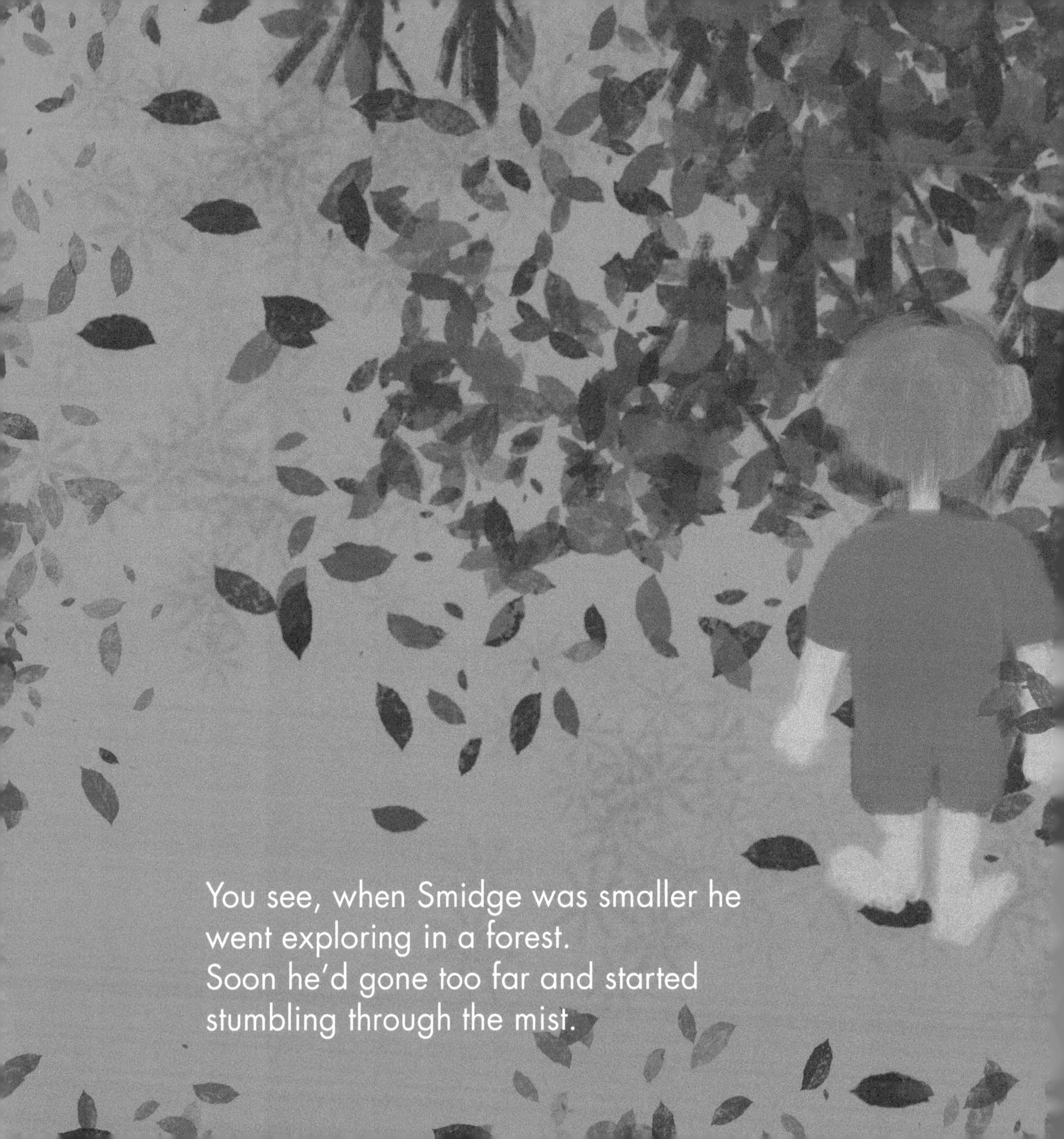

You see, when Smidge was smaller he
went exploring in a forest.
Soon he'd gone too far and started
stumbling through the mist.

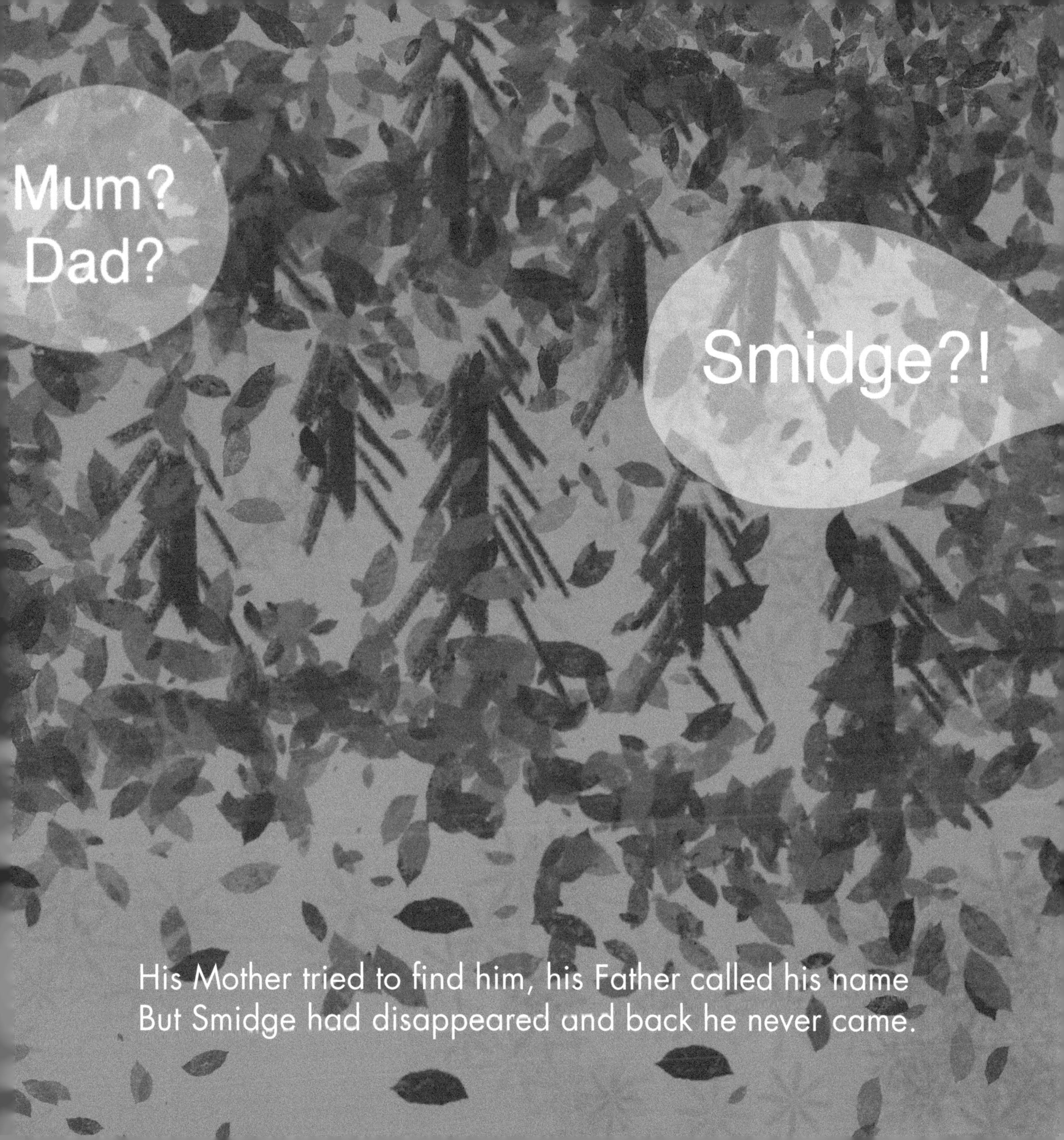
Mum?
Dad?
Smidge?!

His Mother tried to find him, his Father called his name
But Smidge had disappeared and back he never came.

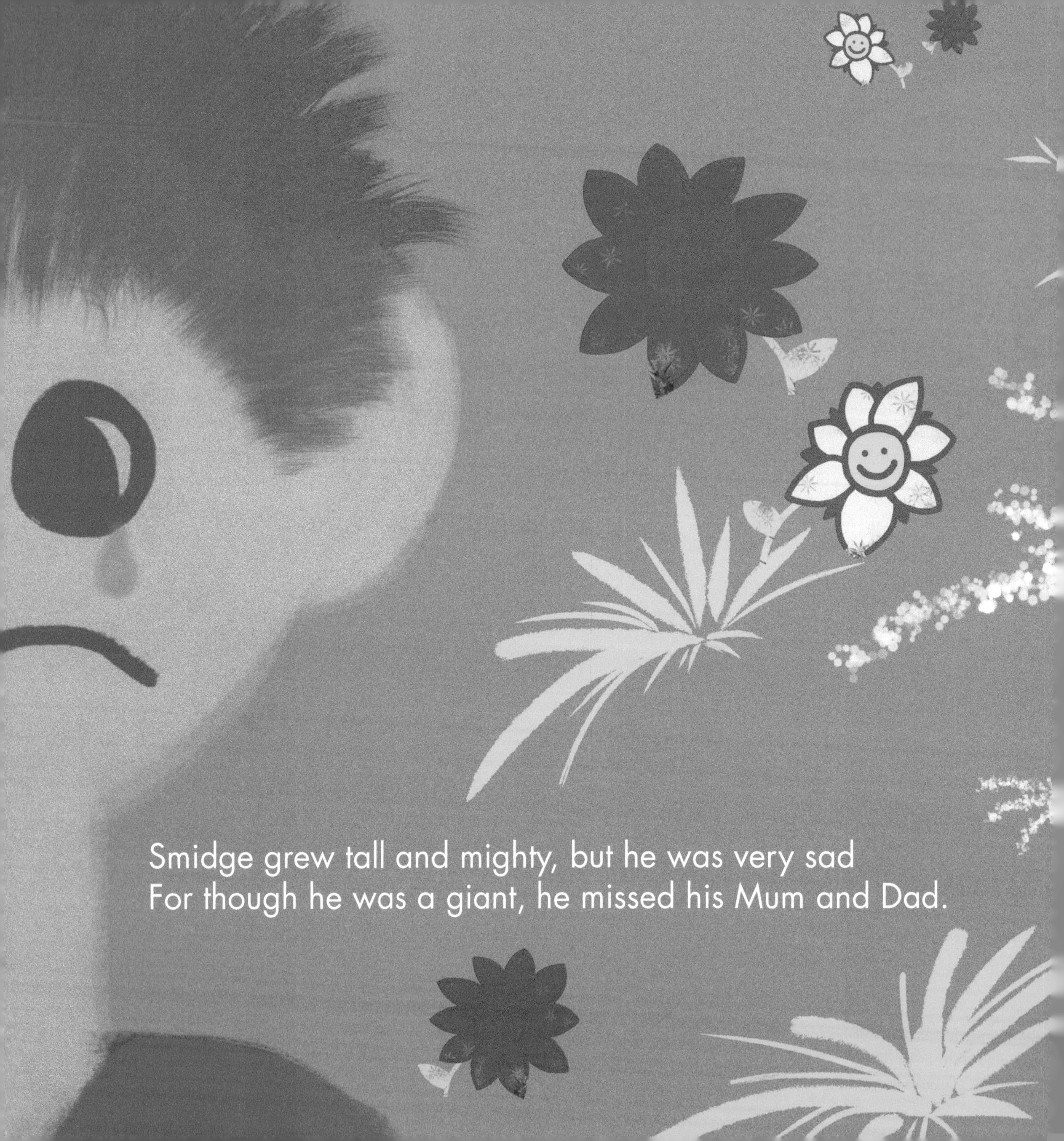

Smidge grew tall and mighty, but he was very sad
For though he was a giant, he missed his Mum and Dad.

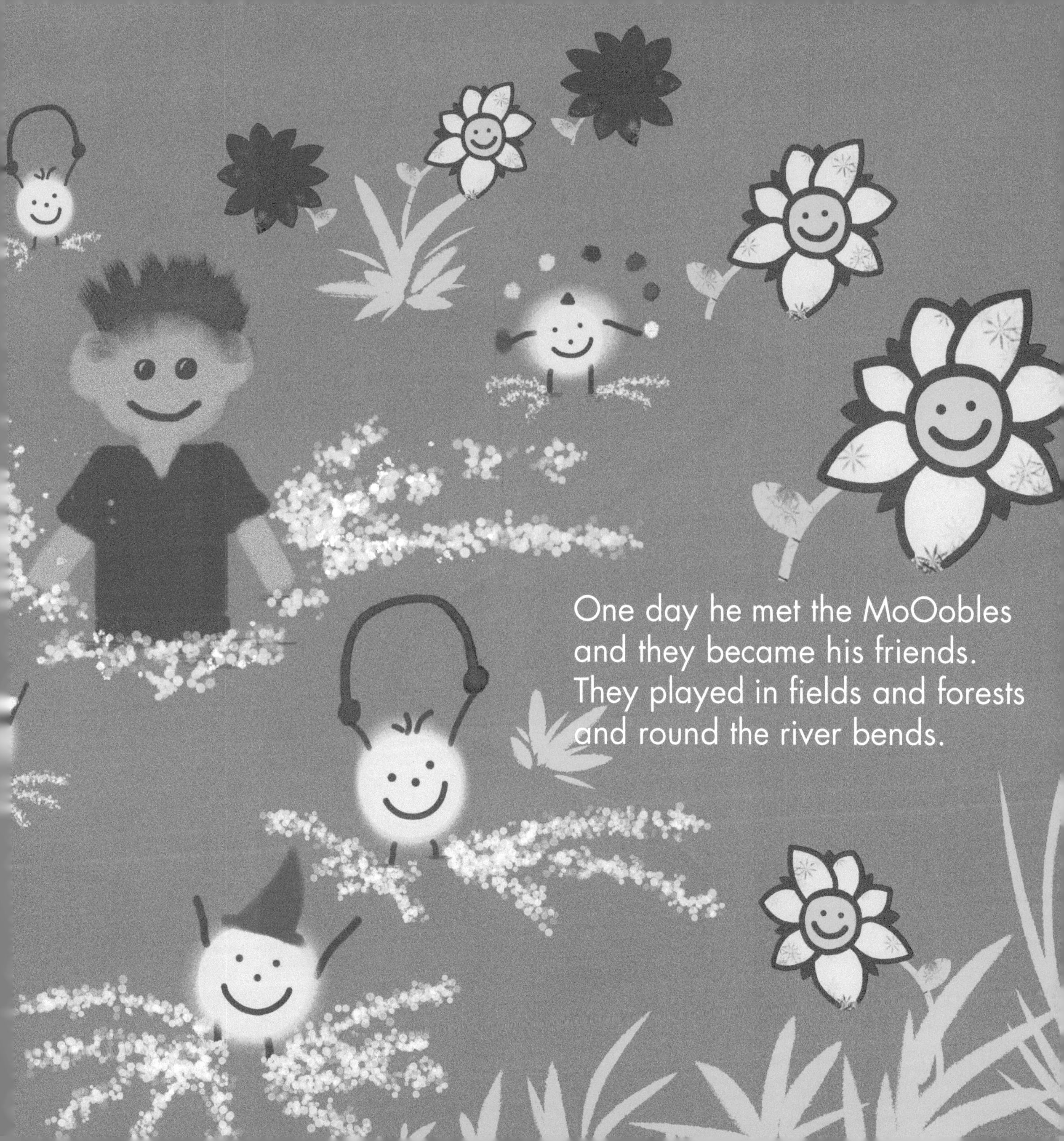

One day he met the MoOobles
and they became his friends.
They played in fields and forests
and round the river bends.

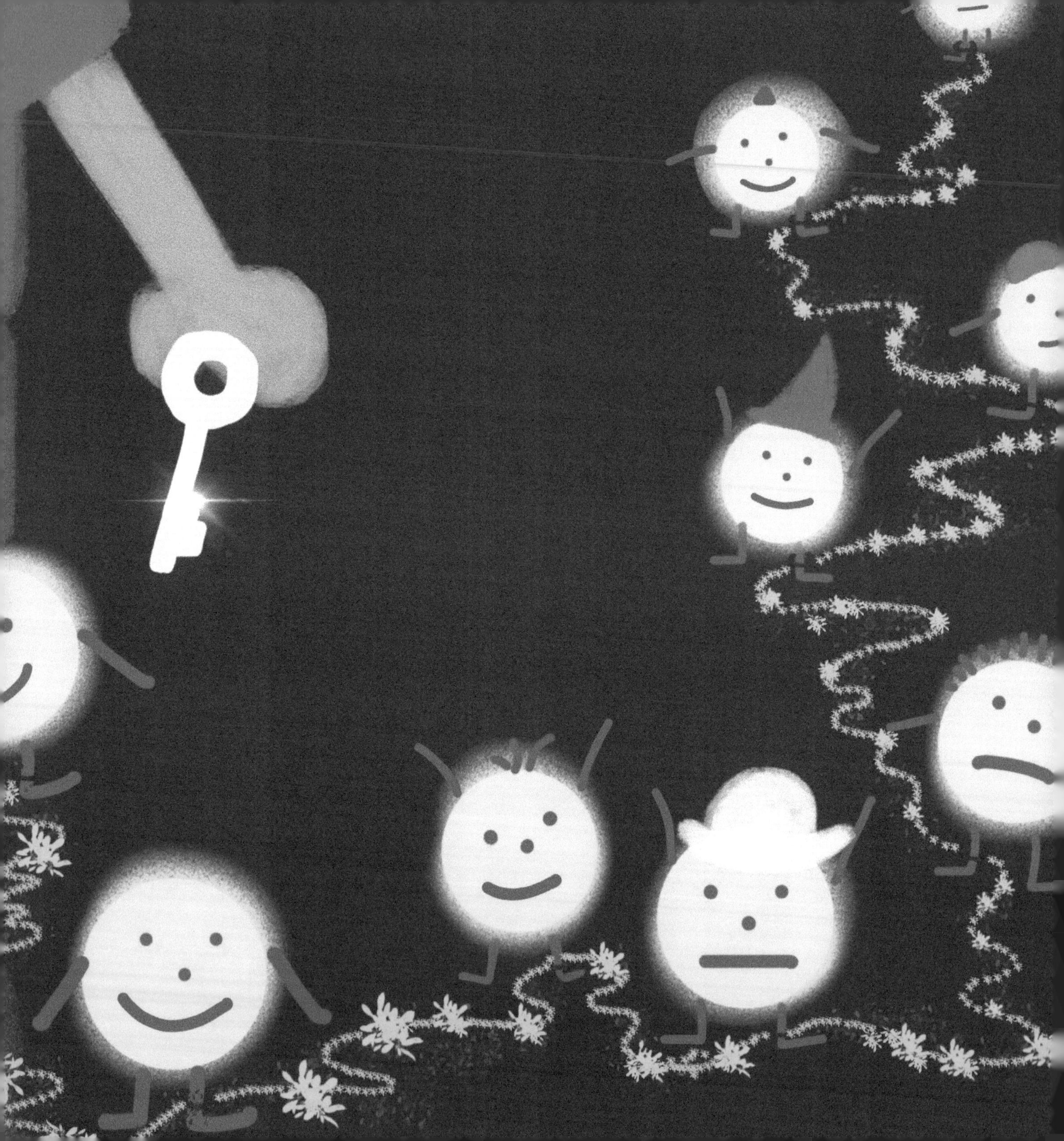

But Smidge kept getting nervous that his new friends might get lost.
He would keep them safe, he thought, at almost any cost.
He tied them all together in one enormous chain
So they could only shuffle up and down and back again.

Smidge thought that this was best and would keep them out of trouble.
He didn't realise how, in fact, he'd made his problems double.
For now the MoOobles could not dance or jump or skip with glee –
They could not play with Smidge like back when they were free.

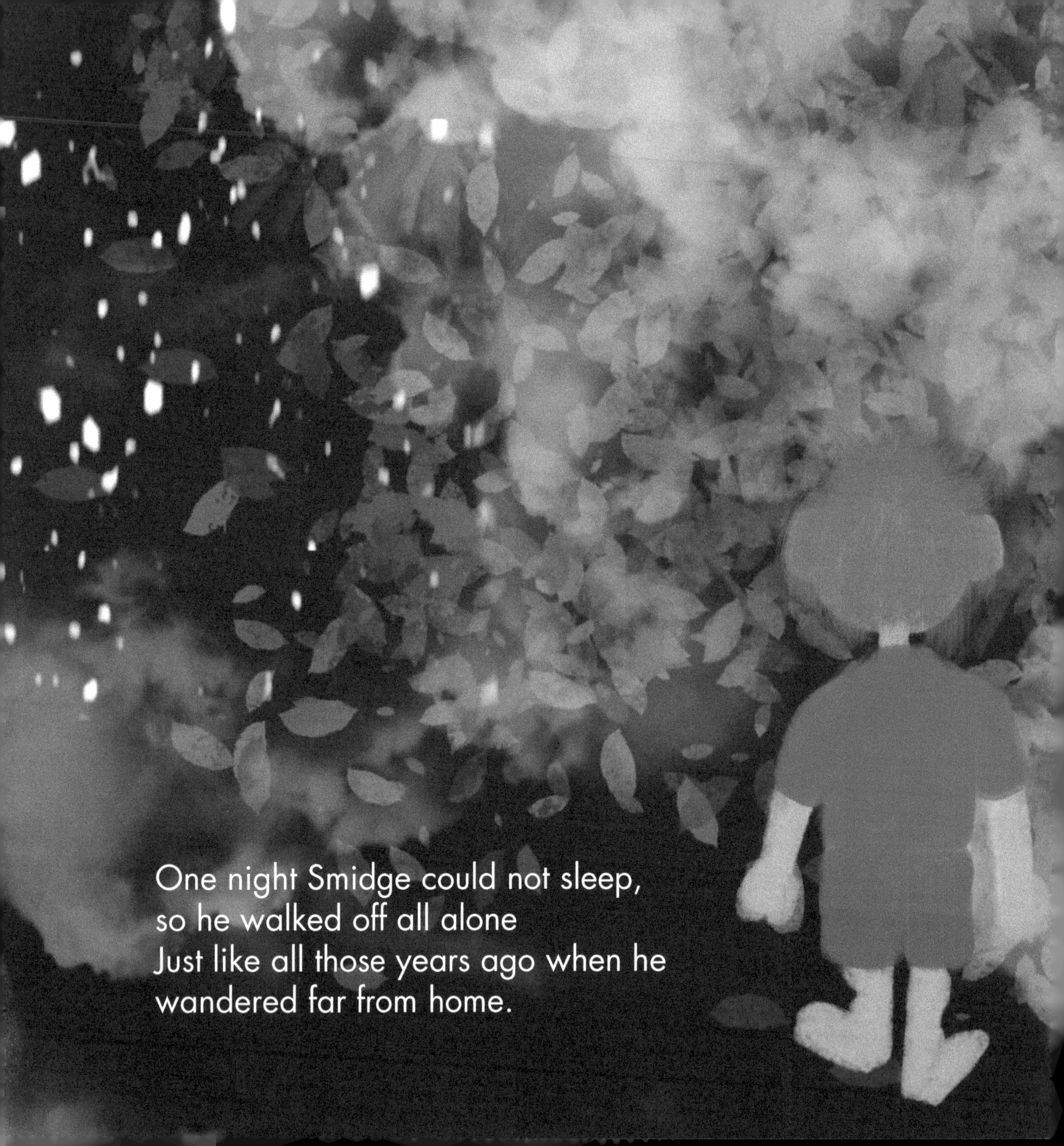

One night Smidge could not sleep,
so he walked off all alone
Just like all those years ago when he
wandered far from home.

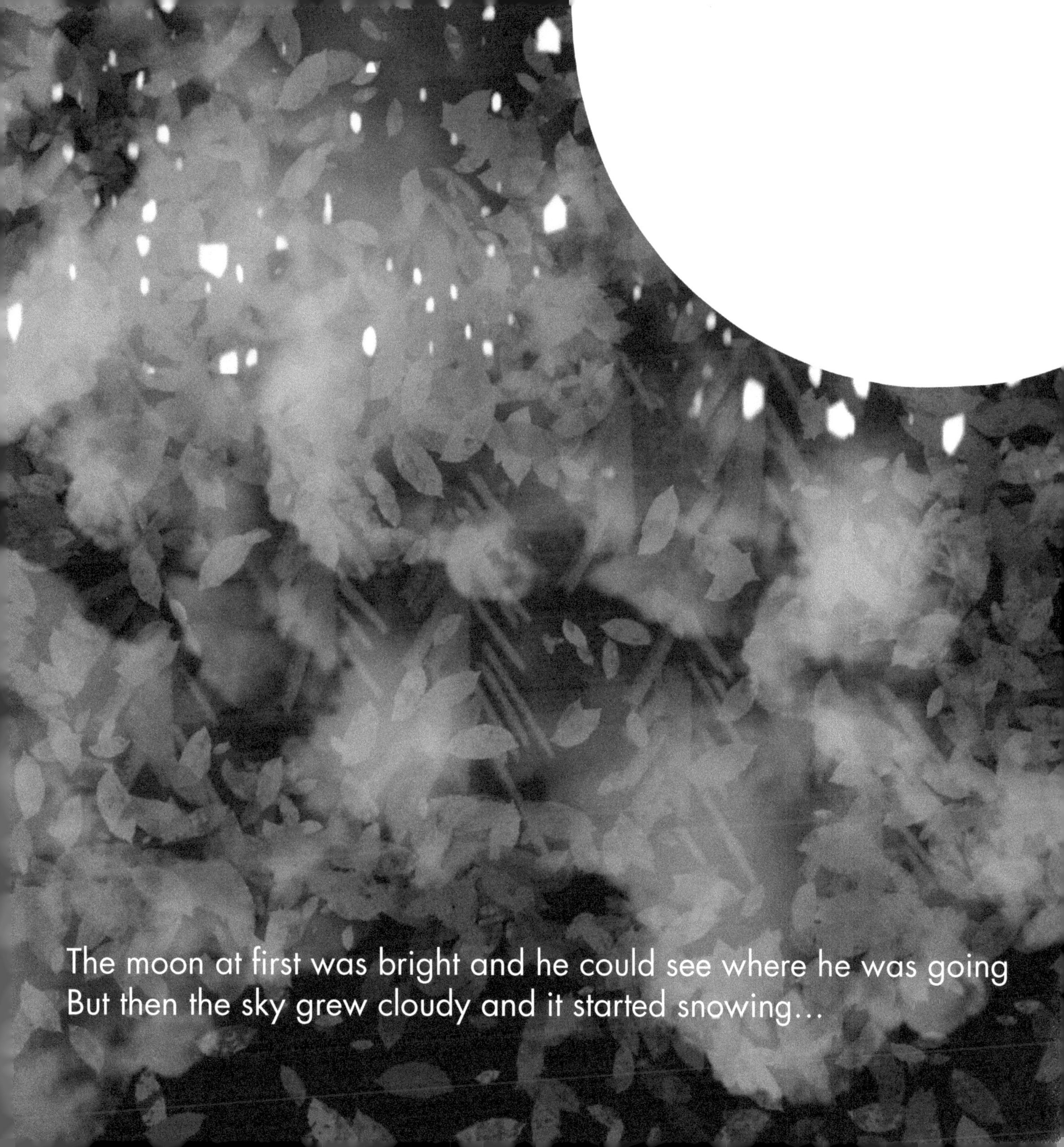

The moon at first was bright and he could see where he was going
But then the sky grew cloudy and it started snowing…

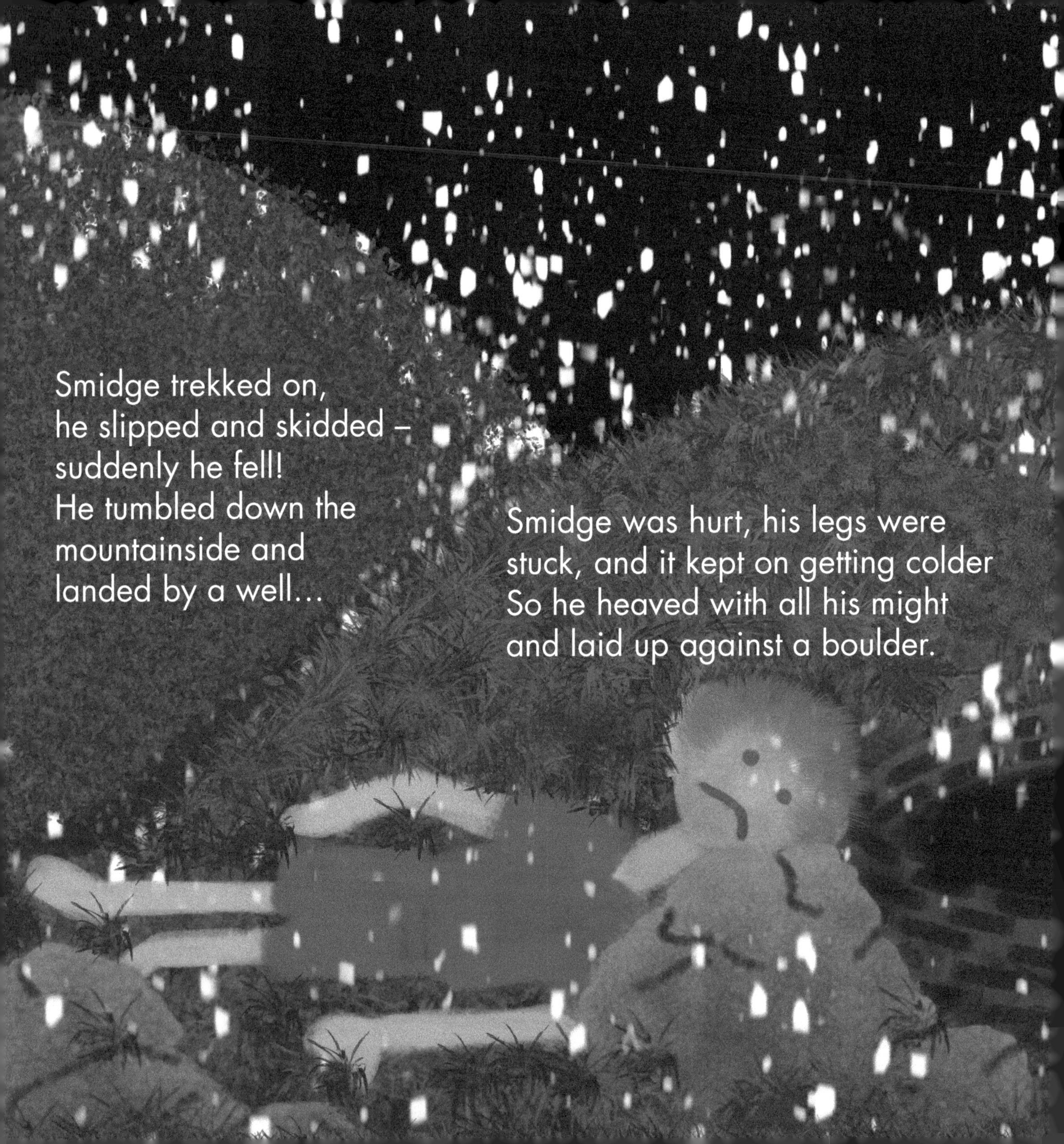

Smidge trekked on,
he slipped and skidded –
suddenly he fell!
He tumbled down the
mountainside and
landed by a well…

Smidge was hurt, his legs were
stuck, and it kept on getting colder
So he heaved with all his might
and laid up against a boulder.

Very soon the Mountain MoOobles noticed Smidge was gone
But they couldn't split up to search for him –
they had to search as one.
Day after day, back and forth, they trekked across the bridge
Shuffling over rocks and rivers, would they ever find poor Smidge?

Then one summer afternoon when they'd almost given up
They had grown quite thirsty, and needed water for their cup.
One MoOoble remembered there was a well not far away

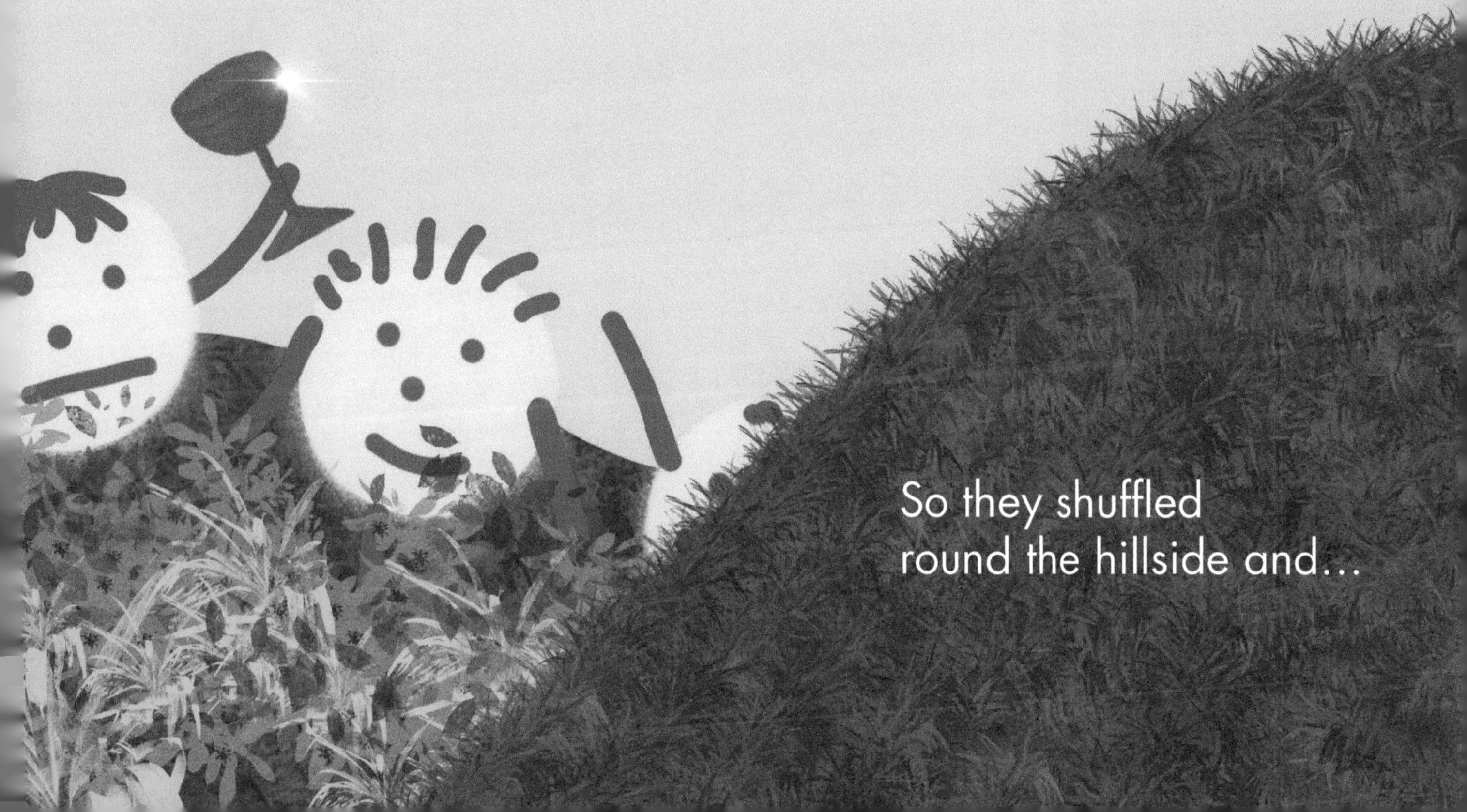

So they shuffled
round the hillside and…

…there was Smidge as clear as day!

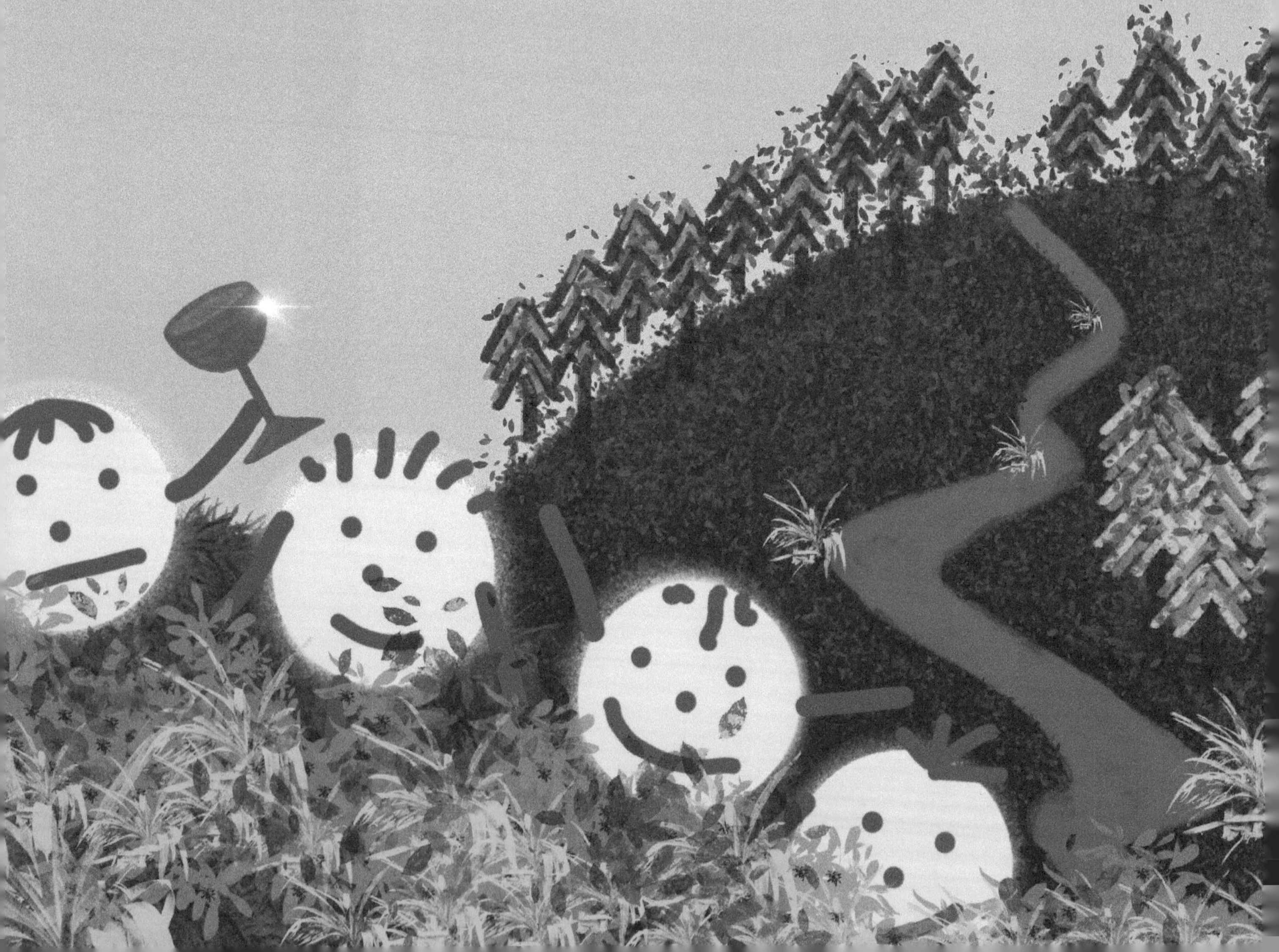

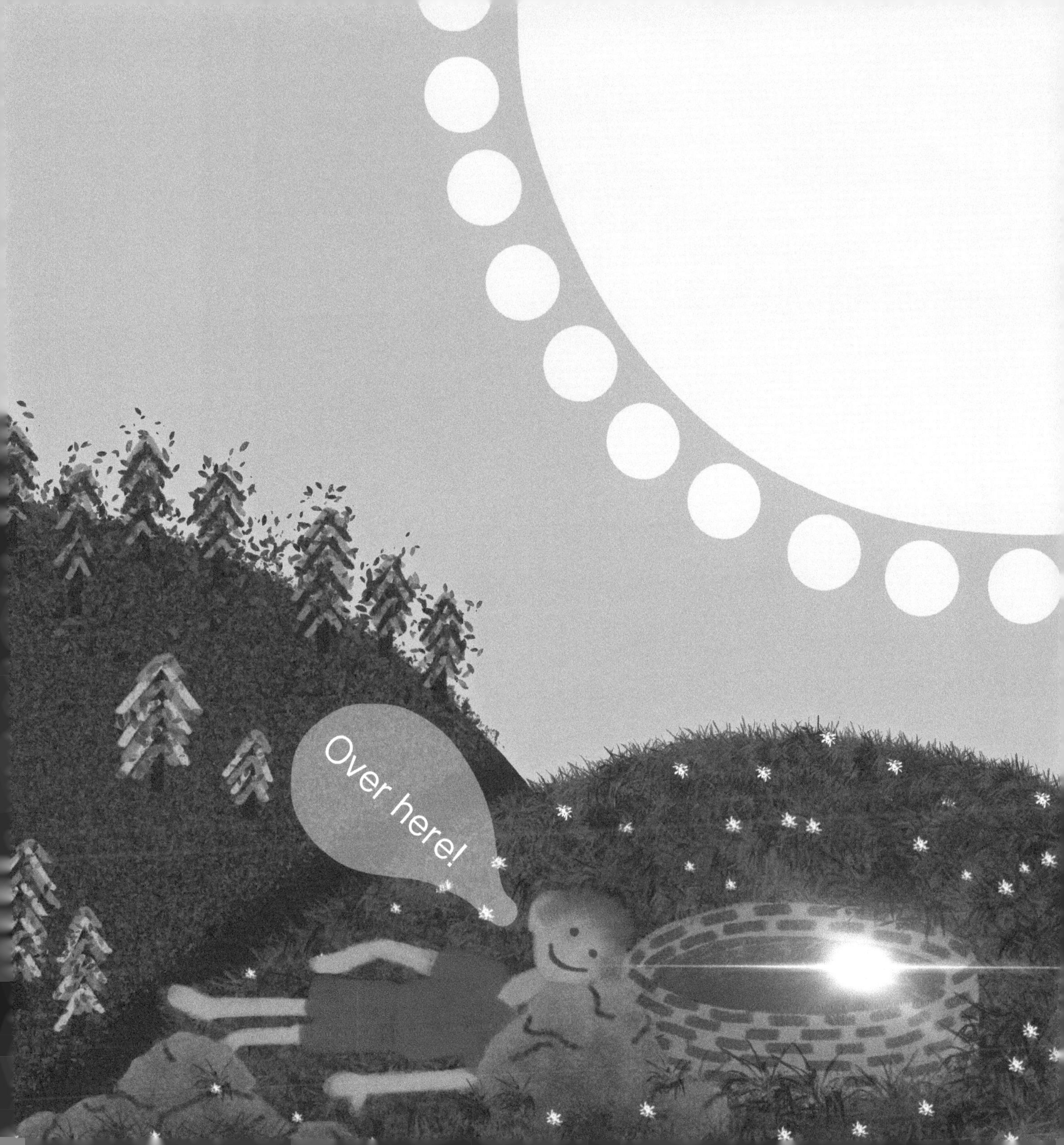
Over here!

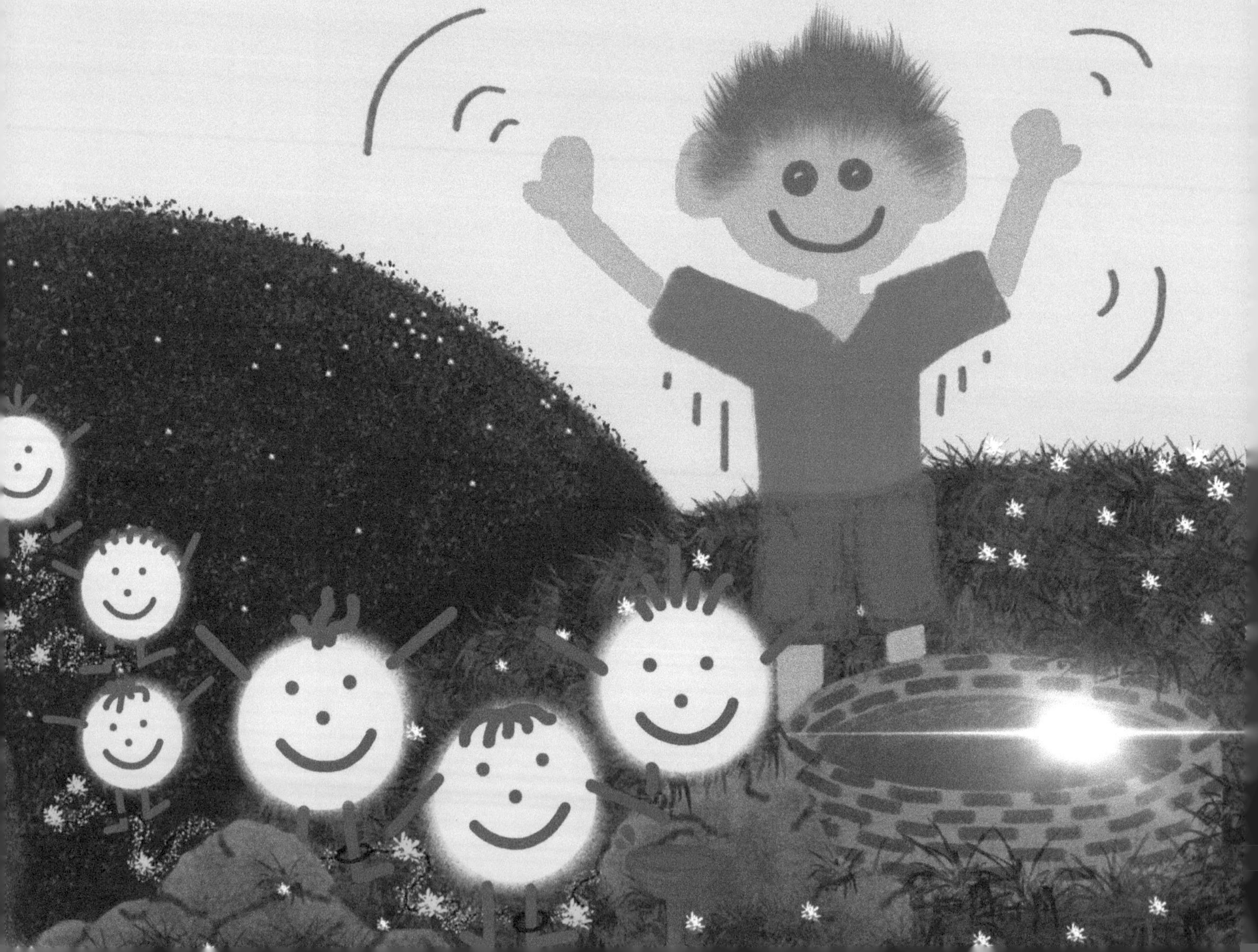

Smidge was overjoyed to see his dearest friends once more!

They set to work to free his legs and helped him from the floor.

He danced and jumped and skipped with glee, laughing –
then he stopped.

He looked down at the MoOobles and his face,
it quickly dropped...

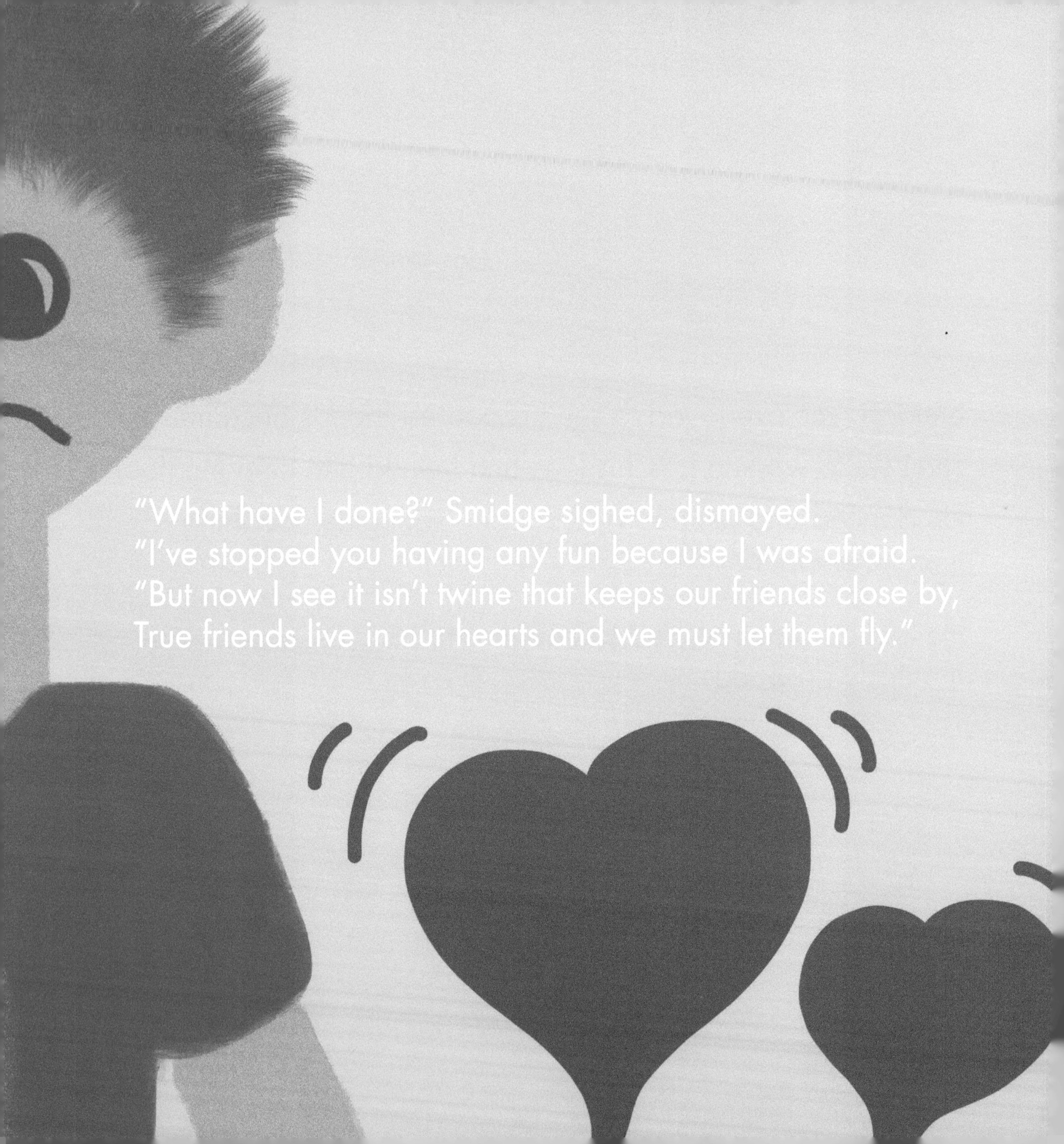

"What have I done?" Smidge sighed, dismayed.
"I've stopped you having any fun because I was afraid.
"But now I see it isn't twine that keeps our friends close by,
True friends live in our hearts and we must let them fly."

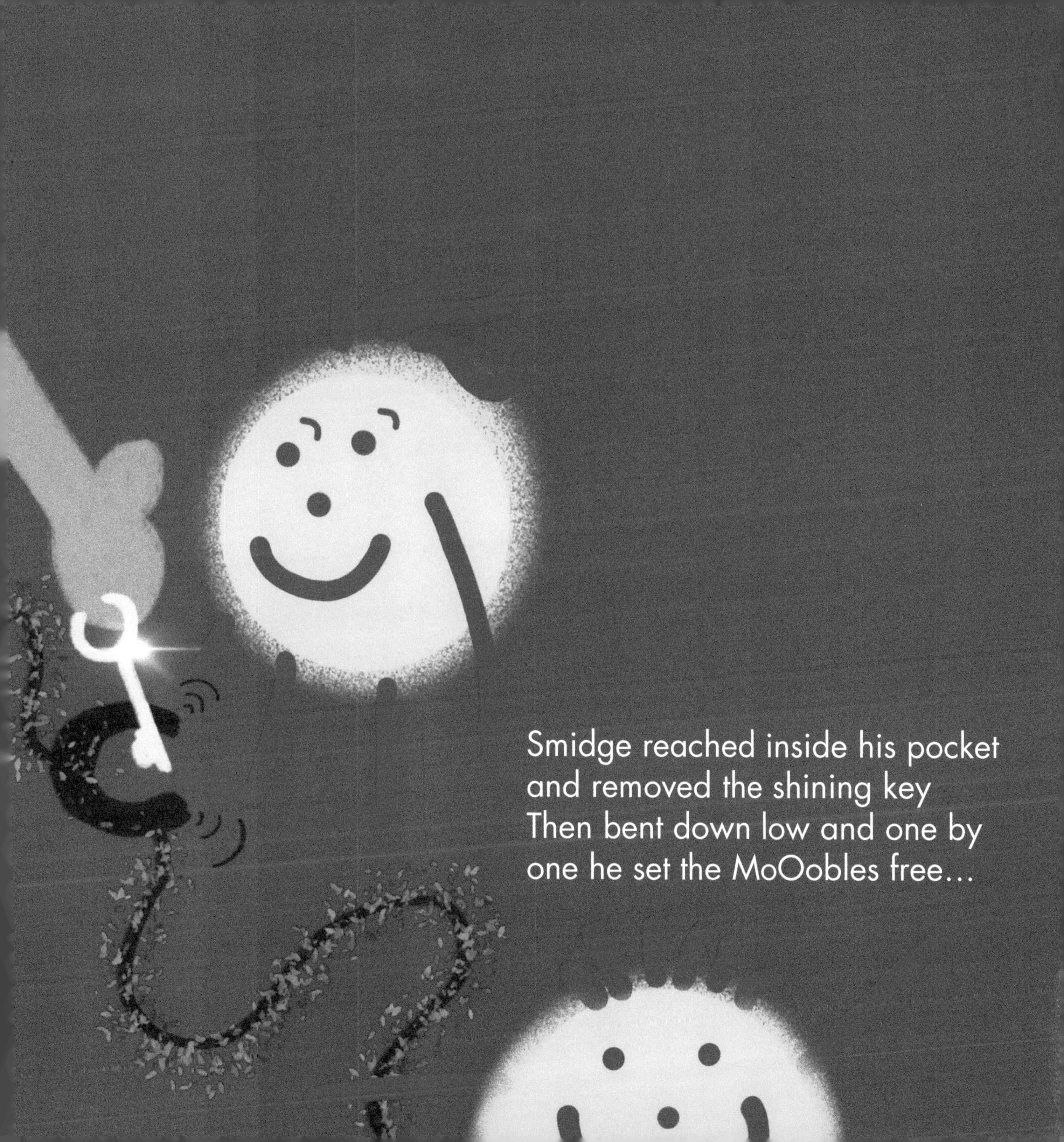

Smidge reached inside his pocket
and removed the shining key
Then bent down low and one by
one he set the MoOobles free...

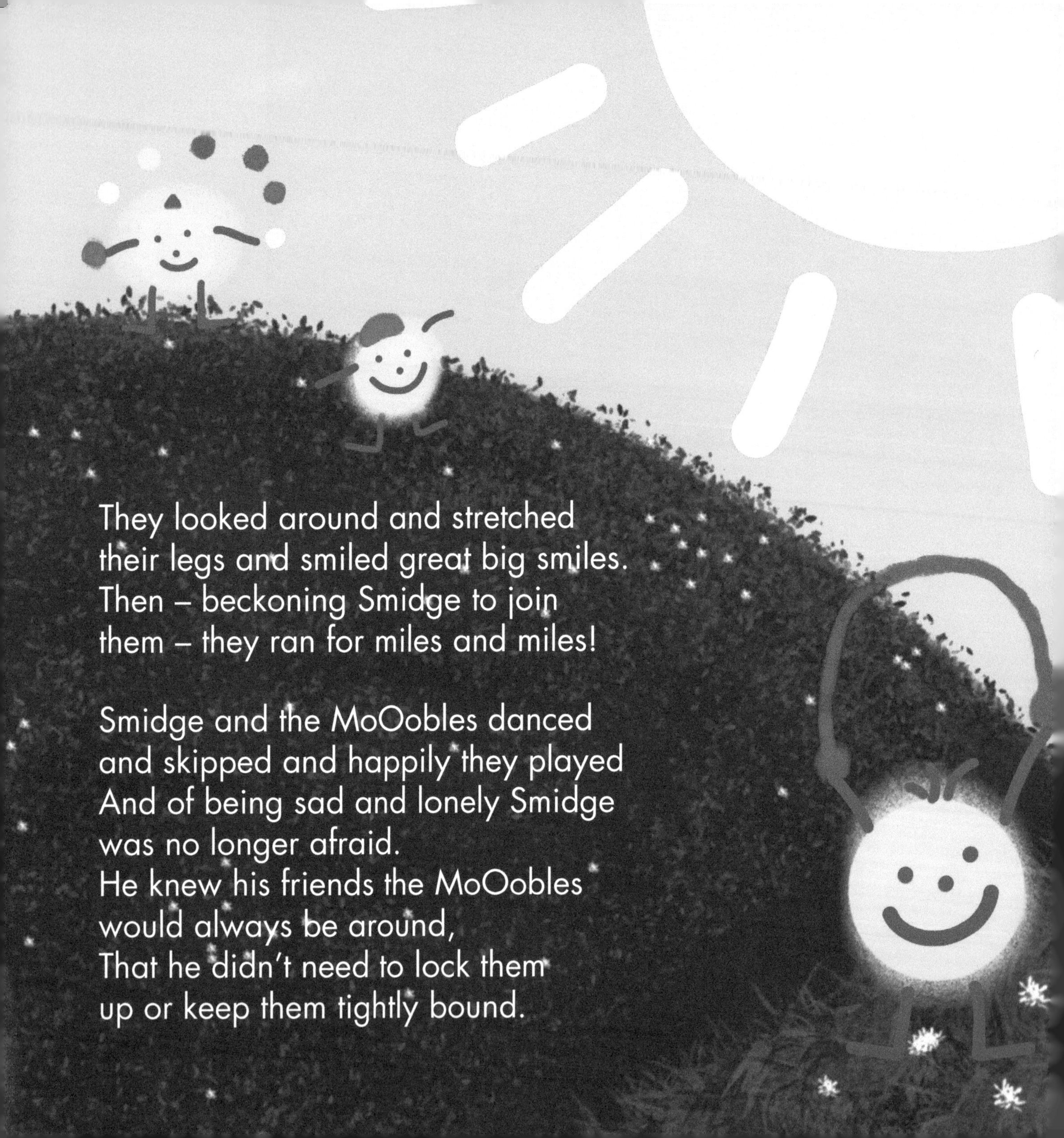

They looked around and stretched
their legs and smiled great big smiles.
Then – beckoning Smidge to join
them – they ran for miles and miles!

Smidge and the MoOobles danced
and skipped and happily they played
And of being sad and lonely Smidge
was no longer afraid.
He knew his friends the MoOobles
would always be around,
That he didn't need to lock them
up or keep them tightly bound.

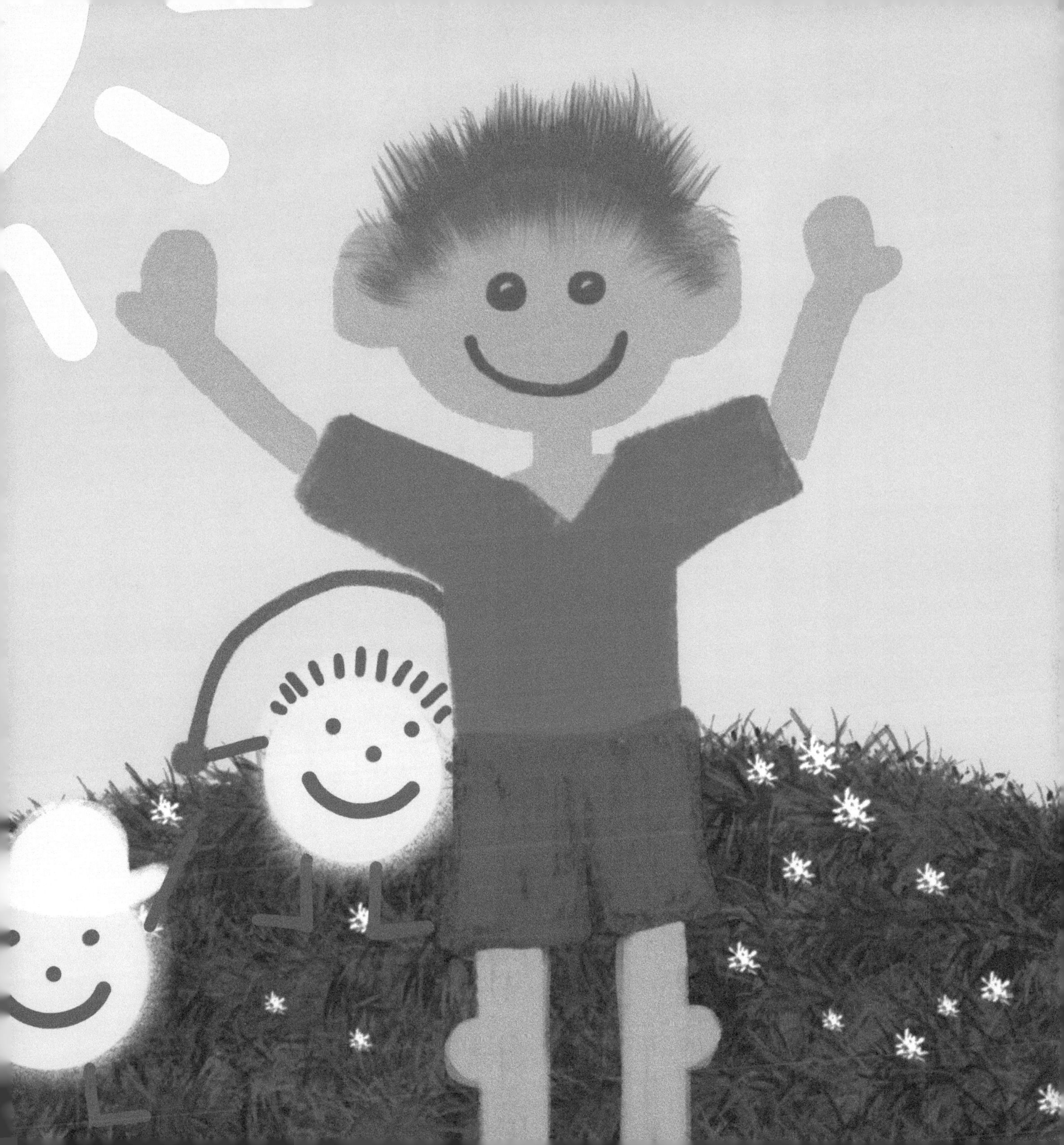

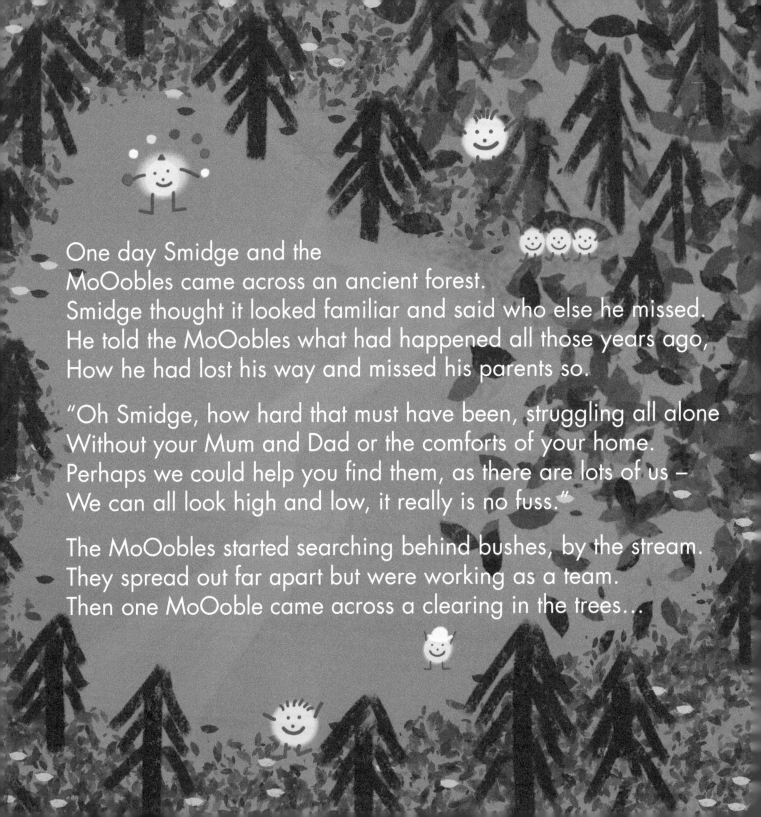

One day Smidge and the
MoOobles came across an ancient forest.
Smidge thought it looked familiar and said who else he missed.
He told the MoOobles what had happened all those years ago,
How he had lost his way and missed his parents so.

"Oh Smidge, how hard that must have been, struggling all alone
Without your Mum and Dad or the comforts of your home.
Perhaps we could help you find them, as there are lots of us –
We can all look high and low, it really is no fuss."

The MoOobles started searching behind bushes, by the stream.
They spread out far apart but were working as a team.
Then one MoOoble came across a clearing in the trees…

And there stood a great big
house made from sticks
and leaves...

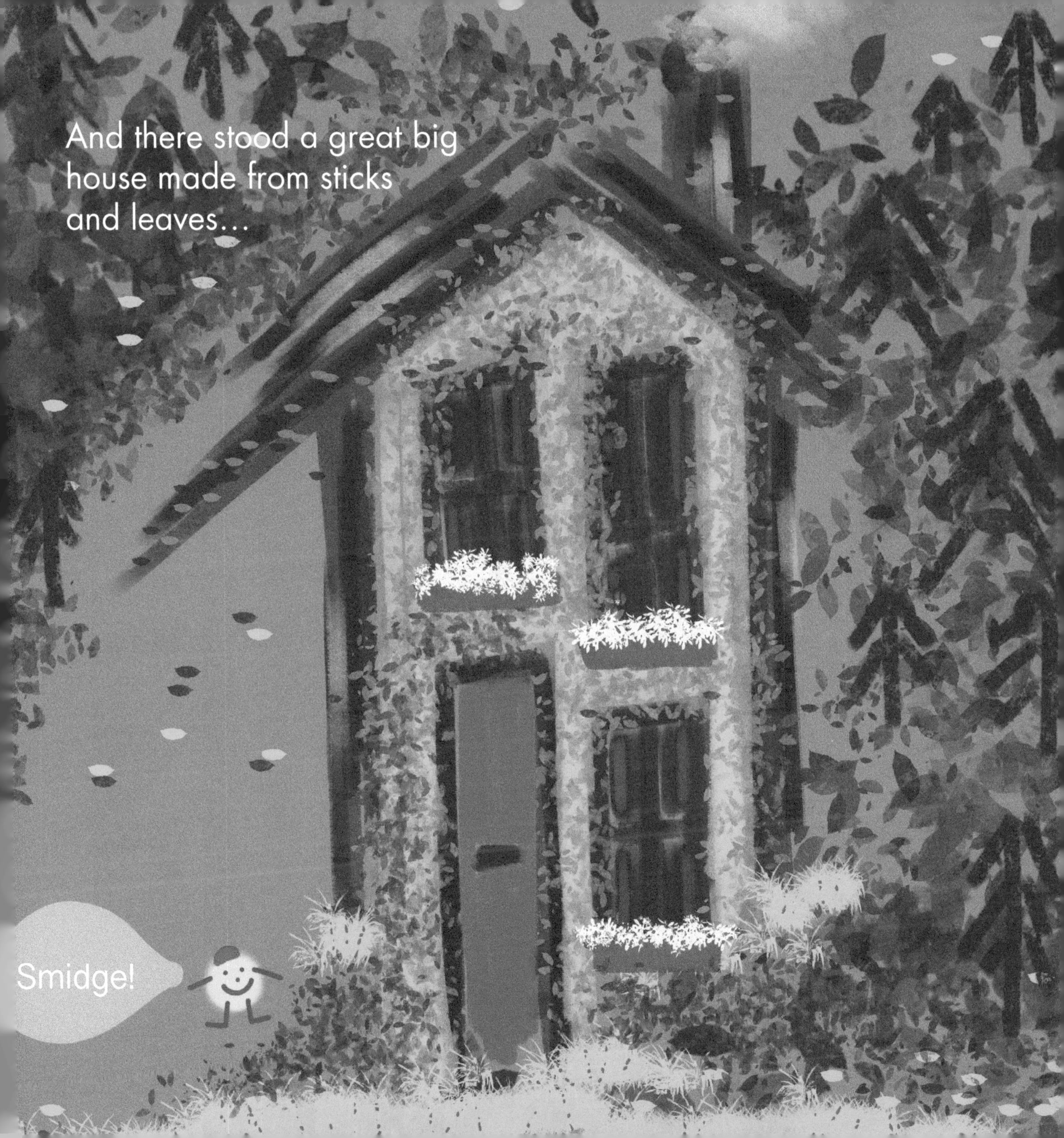
Smidge!

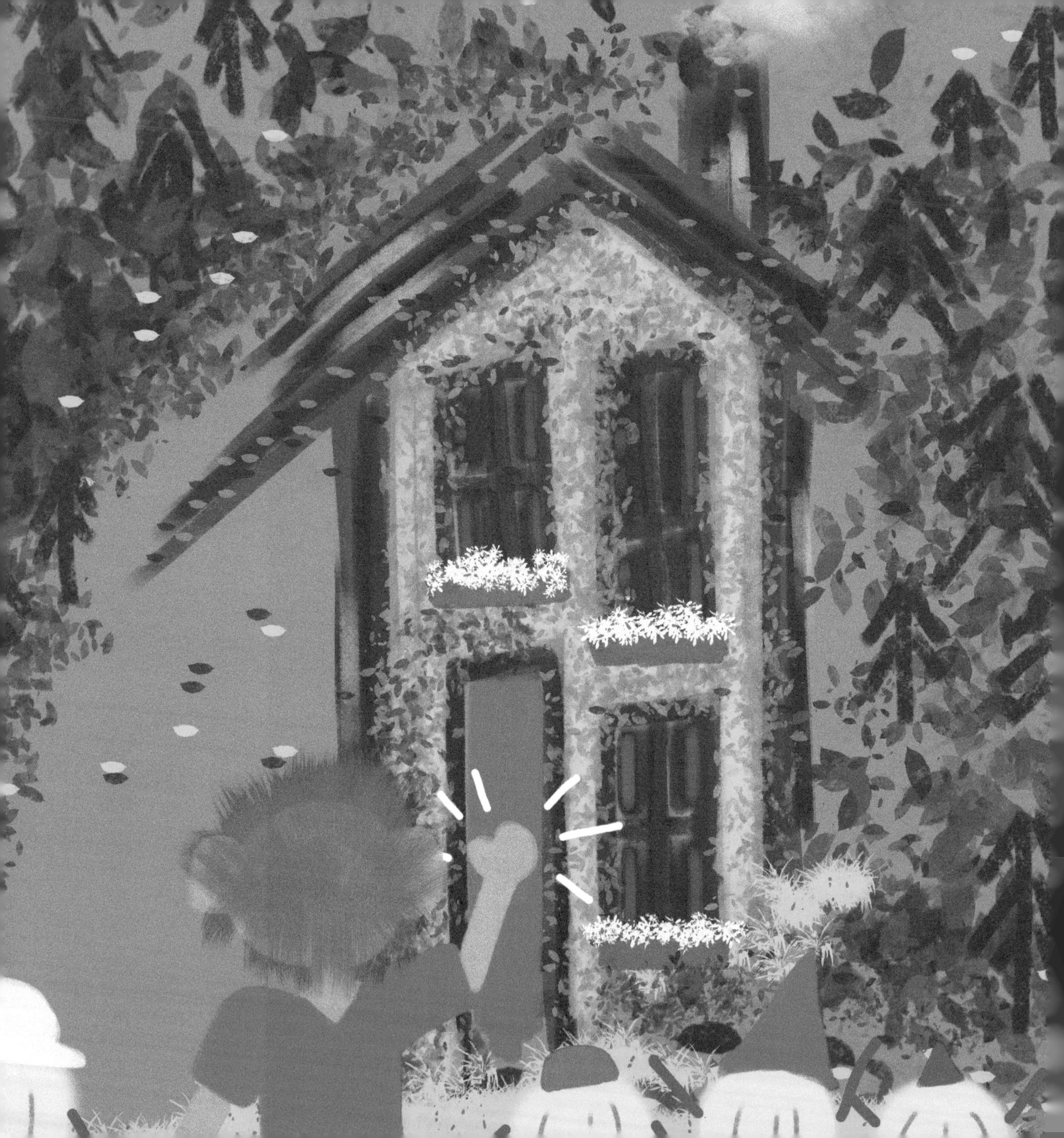

The MoOoble called out loud to Smidge,

"Come quick, I've found a house!

It looks like giants might live here – certainly not a mouse!"

Smidge and the other MoOobles came bounding through the forest.

Smidge stood still, he stopped and looked, and slowly made a fist.

He walked up to the wooden door and tapped it –

knock, knock, knock!

And from inside they all could hear the turning of a lock.

Then the door creaked open, and who was stood inside…?

"Mum and Dad it's really you!"
Smidge gasped out loud and cried.

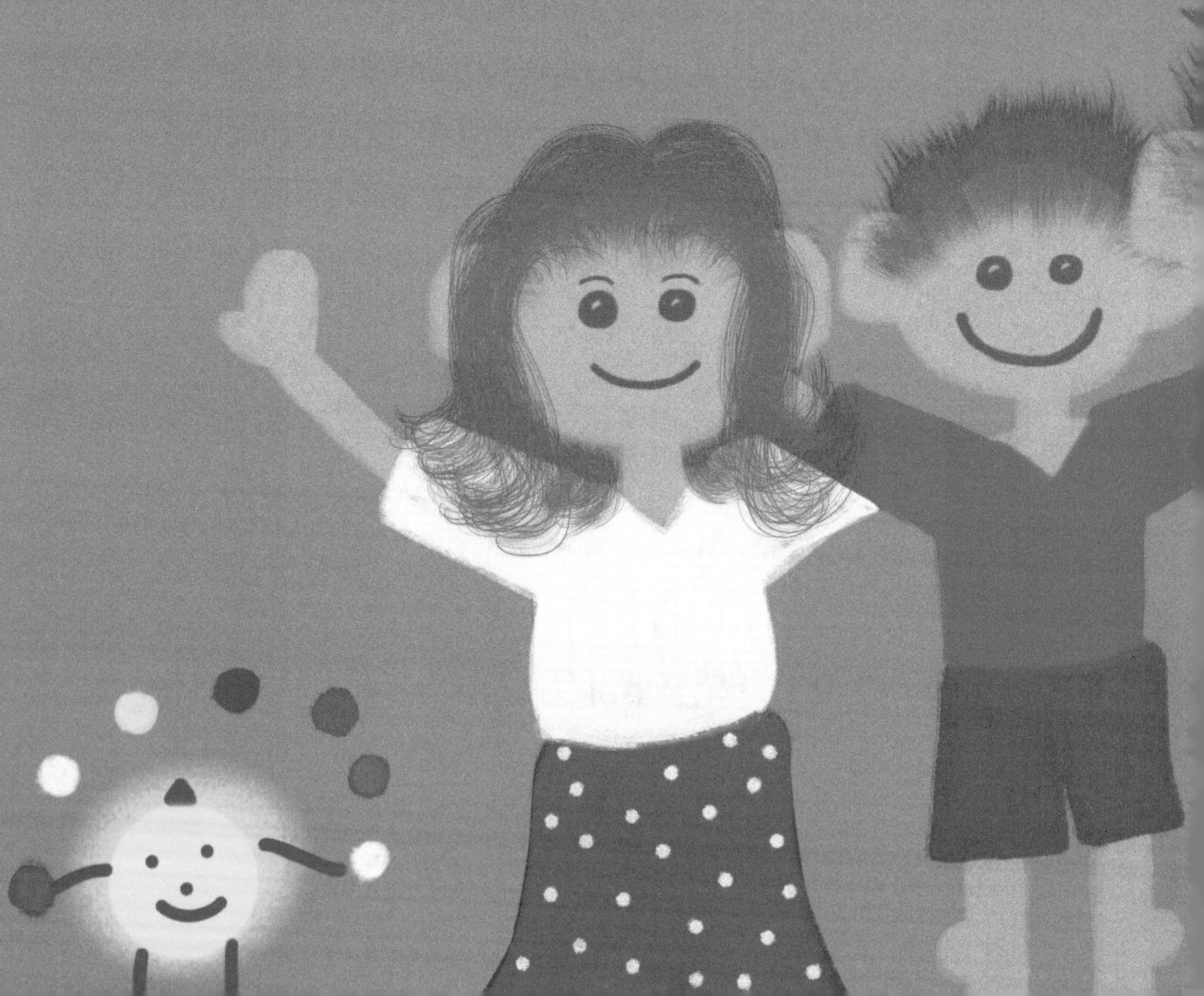

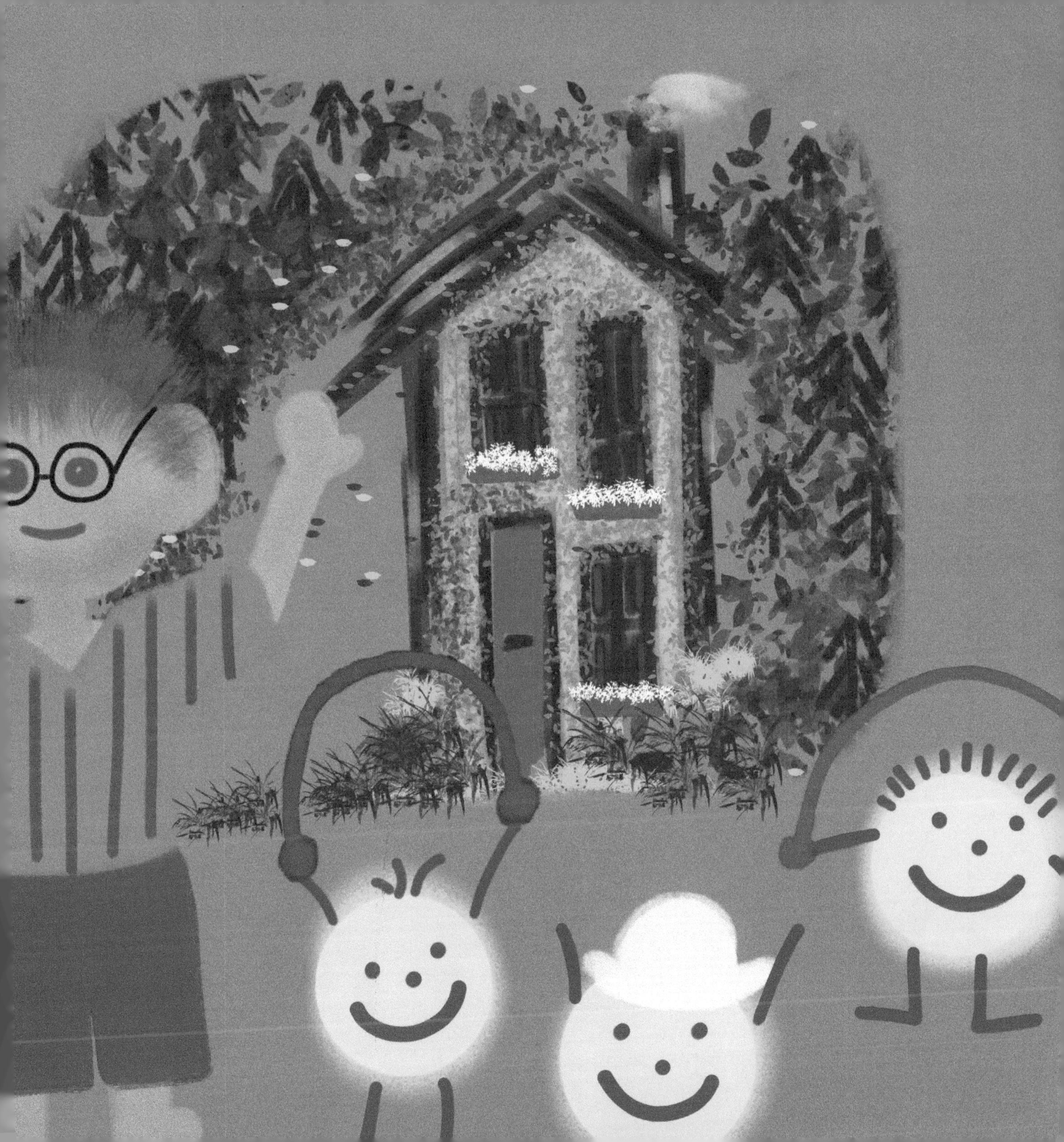

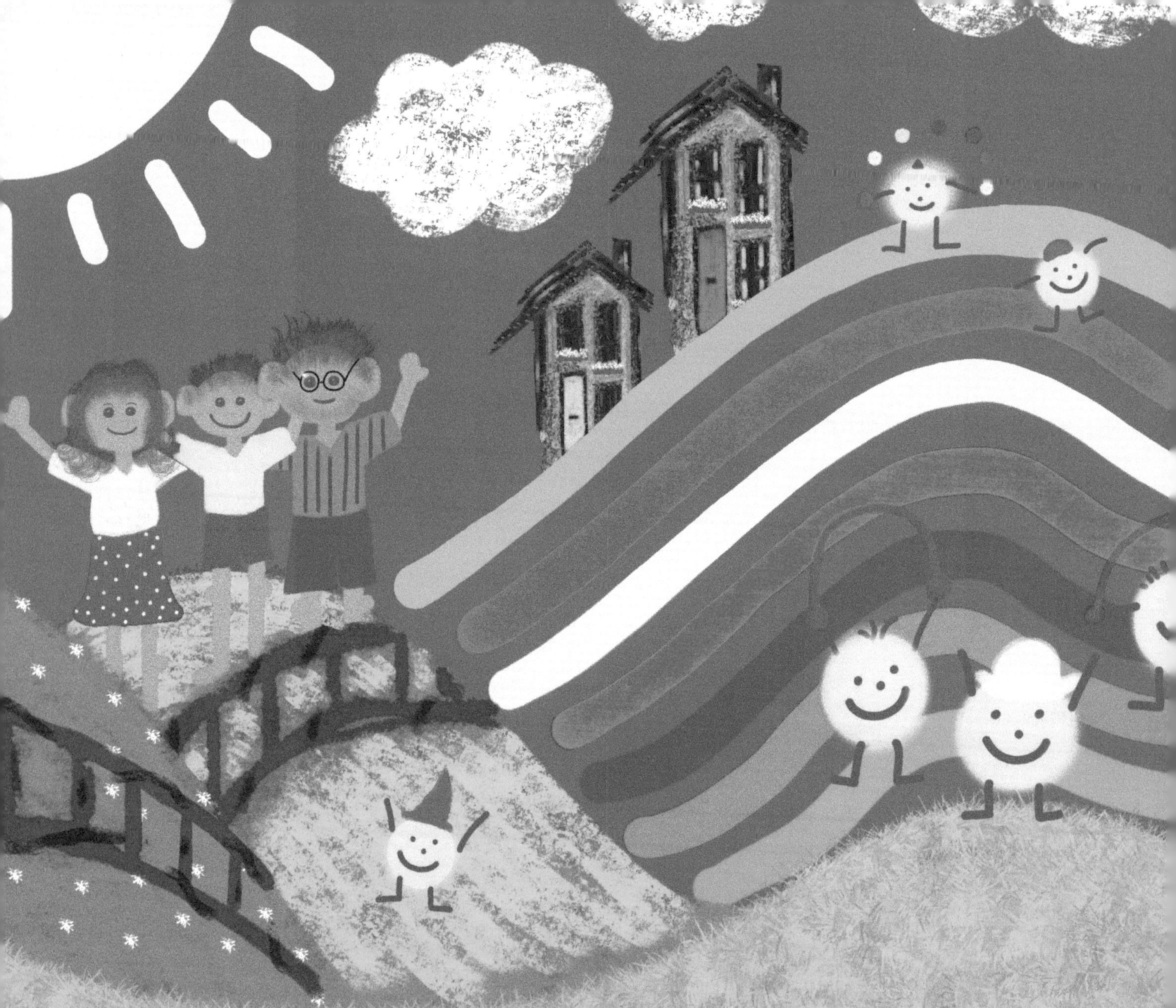

Now Smidge and the MoOobles live next to Smidge's Mum and Dad
On the multi-coloured hillside and they are always glad
That they can happily dance and jump and skip with glee together
Knowing however far they roam, they will always have each other.

Lightning Source UK Ltd.
Milton Keynes UK
UKHW051001190321
380626UK00005B/60